S0-BCY-687

Growing Up Daisy

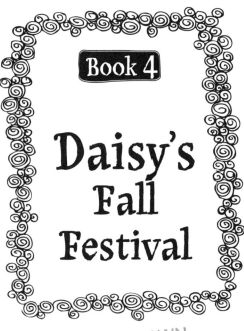

Book 4

Daisy's
Fall
Festival

WITHDRAWN
From the
Mishawaka-Penn-Harris Public Library

By: Marci Peschke
Illustrated by: M.H. Pilz

Mishawaka-Penn-Harris
Public Library
Mishawaka, Indiana

visit us at www.abdopublishing.com

To Para Mis Amigas: Ruby, Vicky & Linda - MP
For Ceci - MHP

Published by Magic Wagon, a division of the ABDO Group, 8000
West 78th Street, Edina, Minnesota 55439. Copyright © 2011 by
Abdo Consulting Group, Inc. International copyrights reserved
in all countries. All rights reserved. No part of this book may
be reproduced in any form without written permission from the
publisher.

Calico Chapter Books™ is a trademark and logo of Magic Wagon.

Printed in the United States of America, Melrose Park, Illinois.
092010
012011
 This book contains at least 10% recycled materials.

Text by Marci Peschke
Illustrated by M.H. Pilz
Edited by Stephanie Hedlund and Rochelle Baltzer
Cover and interior design by Abbey Fitzgerald

Library of Congress Cataloging-in-Publication Data

Peschke, M. (Marci)
   Daisy's fall festival / by Marci Peschke ; illustrated by M.H. Pilz.
      p. cm. -- (Growing up Daisy ; bk. 4)
   ISBN 978-1-61641-117-6
   [1. Festivals--Fiction. 2. Autumn--Fiction. 3. Schools--Fiction. 4.
Mexican Americans--Fiction.] 1. Pilz, MH, ill. 11. Title.
   PZ7.P441245Dc 2011
   [Fic]--dc22
                                   2010028458

Table of Contents

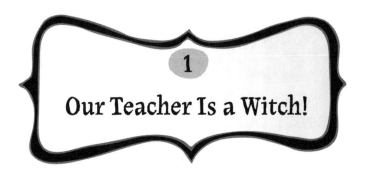

1
Our Teacher Is a Witch!

Daisy Martinez grabbed her best friend Blanca's arm and said, "Oooh, I just love the Fall Festival! I love wearing costumes, playing games, and eating candy apples! What do you think our class should do for a booth at the festival?"

She pointed at the sign in the hall at Townsend Elementary. In big, orange letters it read: Annual Fall Festival ~ Fun For Everyone.

"I don't know yet," Blanca said, "but I'm sure we'll think of something."

"It has to be better than Madison's idea," Daisy said. Just then the warning bell rang. Daisy and Blanca ran down the hall to room 210. They didn't want to be late for class!

The two girls stepped inside room 210. Ms. Lilly was wearing a long, black dress. Her curly black hair looked wild and she had on some extremely pointy black boots.

When she turned around Daisy nearly jumped. Her teacher's face was green in celebration of Halloween. Since their visit to see the King Tut exhibit at the museum, Daisy's class had spent the past five weeks studying holidays. First it was the Chinese New Year, then Valentine's Day, after that St. Patrick's Day, next Cinco de Mayo, and finally Fourth of July.

As usual, Ms. Lilly made everything so much fun! Her class spent hours learning about the Chinese calendar. Daisy was born in the Year of the Ox. And Ms. Lilly got Ms. Pearl, the cafeteria manager, to let them make fortune cookies in the school kitchen.

Min taught Daisy and Blanca how to use chopsticks for their report. For each of the holidays they had learned the history, culture, and traditions related to the celebration. Daisy wondered what Ms. Lilly had in store for Halloween. She didn't have to wait long!

Ms. Lilly said, "Monday we will be having a pumpkin-carving contest, so bring your creative ideas, superstars!" Then she told the class all about jack-o'-lanterns.

Next, she explained about All Saints' Day and All Souls' Day. Then, she gave them some facts about the Day of the Dead.

Daisy and Blanca didn't need to learn about *el dia de la muerte*. Every year both of their families honored the dead in the traditional ways.

Ms. Lilly told the class the plan for the day. She said after lunch she would be reading aloud to them from *The Wizard of Oz*.

"I think the Wicked Witch of the West was really misunderstood. Poor dear!" Ms. Lilly said. "She only had those awful monkeys for friends. You'll see when we get to that part in the book."

Daisy was thinking about another witch. *The Witch of Blackbird Pond* was a book her school librarian, Mrs. Warrick, suggested for her to read. Daisy trusted her librarian and the cover of the book looked good, so she had checked it out.

"Never judge a book by the cover," Mrs. Warrick liked to say, "or you might miss a real adventure."

After the story, Ms. Lilly had them do an activity with nouns, verbs, adjectives, and adverbs. Next, they had their D.E.A.R. (Drop Everything and Read) time. Then, they filled out their reading journals.

Finally, it was time to go to art. Raymond really liked art. He said, "Art is my best subject, besides lunch."

Raymond sat behind Daisy in class. He had given her a special souvenir when they went to the museum. After that Blanca said, "Raymond likes you, Daisy!"

Daisy thought Blanca was being *tonta*. But then she started to notice that Raymond was always willing to share one of his lunches with *her*. He never offered nachos or pizza to any of the other kids at the table.

Today, they would have art with Min's class. Ms. Browner was the art teacher. She said, "You can always remember my name because it has the color brown in it. Isn't that great? I just love colors." She really did, too.

The art room was a large, sunny room with lots of windows. Ms. Browner had painted two of the walls a sunny yellow and two of the walls a bright sky blue.

Pictures of famous paintings, vases of sunflowers, and interesting sculptures were everywhere you looked. Ms. Browner liked to inspire young artists.

Maps of South America and Mexico were on the wall. Daisy noticed on one counter there were small carved and painted animals. She had seen them in Oaxaca, Mexico, when her family visited relatives there.

Ms. Browner had written the words *Folk Art* on the whiteboard. Under those words, their art teacher had written the names Diego Rivera and Frida Kahlo. She explained that the artists were married to each other. Diego painted murals. Frida created paintings.

At the end of art class, Ms. Browner gave the students choices for an art project that would be due the next Friday. Students could work in a group on a mural, or individually on a painting, pot, or carving.

"I'm carving a frog," Raymond said.

Madison, Lizzie, and Amber were going to paint a mural. Daisy and Min decided to paint a picture.

"I will make a pot," Blanca said. "I think I might be the only kid making one."

Daisy said, "Hey, that's kind of cool. I bet lots of kids choose painting."

Ms. Lilly was at the door calling, "All of my superstar students, come and line up for lunch." Everyone was talking in the hall. They were so excited about the Folk Art projects.

Ms. Lilly stopped the line. "I would rather be a cheerleader than a cop, so cool it, kiddos. The noise stops now!" she said in her toughest voice.

Everyone stopped talking. No one wanted to disappoint Ms. Lilly, not even Madison. They stopped at room 210 and some kids went in to get their lunch boxes. Daisy grabbed hers.

Blanca saved Daisy a place in line. Then, they walked down the hall to the cafeteria. On the way, Daisy saw another poster. It said: *Come to the Annual Fall Festival!*

Daisy pointed to it and Blanca nodded. They would talk about it some more at lunch, but right now they were trying to be super quiet.

2

Calacas Are Cool

At lunch, everyone was talking about art and the Fall Festival. When DeShaye and Min walked up, DeShaye said, "Hey, what's up?"

"We're trying to think of a booth for the festival," Daisy replied. "Do you have any ideas?"

Min told them all about Ms. Smith's batting cage. She thought the boys would like it. DeShaye was complaining because her class was doing a cakewalk.

"Can you believe it?" she asked.

Blanca said, "I believe it! Hey, they have pizza today!"

Min looked inside her lunch box and said, "I have sushi rolls."

Daisy looked in hers and said, "I have tortilla rolls." Then they both laughed. Without planning it, they seemed to have almost the same lunch every day!

As the kids ate, they talked about the art project assignment Ms. Browner had given them. Daisy said, "I can't wait to start painting."

From the other end of the table, Raymond bragged, "My frog will be the best." Then he offered Daisy some pizza.

"No thanks, Raymond," Daisy said.

Ever since Blanca told her that Raymond liked her, Daisy was careful not to take food from him every day. She liked him, but not as a boyfriend.

Abuela had put cinnamon *churros* in her lunch today, probably because it was Friday. She put in extra for Daisy to share. Ever since Abuela brought them on the field trip, everyone kept asking Daisy to bring churros, even Madison.

Daisy had been worried that the kids in her class would make fun of Abuela. But when she had chaperoned them on the trip, they all thought she was cool.

"Who wants churros?" Daisy asked. Kids began to shout, "I want some!"

"I know Abuela sent extra for me," Raymond said. He was right, too. When Daisy's abuela found out Raymond's grandma had died, she has been sending him treats. Churros were his favorite.

Daisy asked Blanca, "So what do you think our class should do for the Fall Festival?"

Frowning, Blanca said, "We always have the same old things every year! We need to think of something really different."

"I've been thinking about it all morning, too," Daisy said. "I think we should do something with *calacas*!"

Calacas were skeletons that were dressed up just like they were still living. There were

mariachi calacas, farmer calacas, and even bride and groom calacas.

Blanca gasped, "Ooooh, I love it! What can we do with calacas?"

"I'm still working on that part," Daisy said with a shrug.

DeShaye groaned, "You'll think of something awesome and I'll be giving away cakes!"

Min suggested, "Be sure it's something to do and not just to see or eat. Everyone likes to do something fun at festivals."

Daisy and her friends didn't know that Madison and her friends were talking about the same thing at their table. In fact, Madison had already started to tell everyone they would be having a bake sale in room 210.

After lunch, Ms. Lilly read from *The Wizard of Oz* again. She stopped right where Dorothy's house landed on the witch.

"Please read a little more," Raymond begged, "so we can find out if the house killed her!"

Ms. Lilly smiled and put the book on her desk. She said, "Tomorrow I will read some more, Raymond. Right now we have an afternoon of learning ahead of us.

"Okay, superstars, I'm putting you in groups. Each group will study an October holiday. You are going to use the information you find to write a little book about Halloween, All Saints' Day, All Souls' Day, or the Day of the Dead."

Ms. Lilly showed an example of a little book she made for Valentine's Day. It was amazing!

She went on to explain that the books would need a dedication, table of contents, illustrations, and at least five chapters.

When the books were done, Ms. Lilly would bind them. Mrs. Warrick, their librarian, had agreed to display them in the library!

After she asked them to choose a partner for their book project, Ms. Lilly had one more surprise for them. She walked around the room with a brown paper sack. Then she said, "Daisy, I will start with you. Stick your hand in the bag and choose a topic."

Daisy put her hand in the bag. Her brown eyes opened wide with amazement. Daisy thought there would be slips of paper in the bag, but instead she felt funny shapes. Some were pointy and some were smooth. Some seemed to be round and one felt almost like a plus sign.

Daisy swirled them around and pulled out a pumpkin. Ms. Lilly said, "Fantastic! You and Blanca will be researching Halloween."

Madison got angel wings, which meant she and Lizzie got All Saints' Day. Some kids got crosses for All Souls' Day, and others got skulls for the Day of the Dead.

Ms. Lilly said, "Students, please sign up to use our class computers, go to the library, or borrow encyclopedias. You will have one hour to work on your projects today. They will be due next week."

Daisy asked Blanca to get the encyclopedias. While they flipped through the pages, Daisy told Blanca all about her little sister's birthday party. The party was Saturday afternoon at the party pavilion at Shady Bend Park.

The pavilion was a roof that covered ten large picnic tables. Her parents had invited all of their relatives. Paola had invited her whole class to her party. Daisy had asked Paola if Blanca could come too, and she'd said yes.

Daisy was the oldest kid in her family. Even her cousins were younger. Daisy said, "Blanca, please tell me you are coming to the *fiesta*! If you don't I won't have anyone to hang out with."

Daisy pushed the open World Book Encyclopedia across the desk so Blanca could see the page.

Blanca replied, "You know I'm coming. I love Paola! She seems just like my kid sister too, the way she follows us around all the time."

Daisy smiled. She sighed, "I knew you would be there for me. Look, they have trick-or-treating in here. Are you going trick-or-treating this year?"

Flipping the page, Daisy stopped and pointed at the page excitedly. She said, "Fortune-telling is in here, too! Don't you think our booth would be the coolest and most popular if we did fortune-telling for the festival?"

Blanca replied, "That would be awesome!"

Daisy couldn't wait to tell Ms. Lilly and all the kids in her class. Both girls forgot all about trick-or-treating.

The bell rang and Daisy ran to the shelf to put away the books they were using. Over her shoulder she said to Blanca, "I'll call you tonight and we can plan it all out before we say anything to the class!"

Daisy's mind was bursting with possibilities for their fortune-telling idea. If she had a crystal ball right now she would look into it and see if her class would love her idea as much as she did.

She thought everyone would line up to hear their fortune told. Everyone at Townsend Elementary already thought Ms. Lilly had superpowers.

Daisy shoved her books in her backpack, walked out of the classroom, and then rushed out the front doors of the school. Looking up, she saw a perfect blue sky and decided it was going to be a really fun Fall Festival after all.

3

Paola's Fiesta

When Daisy got home from school, she could barely see her abuela's white braids peeking over a pile of tissue paper flowers.

Abuela said, "Is that you, *mi ja*? Come and help me with these flowers for Paola's fiesta."

Daisy dropped her backpack on the floor, sat down at the table, and began to fold some hot pink tissue paper to make a flower. There were already some from every color in the rainbow on the table.

Soon, her brothers came in shouting. Manuel said, "Abuela, what can we eat for a snack?"

Abuela pointed to a bowl of fruit on the counter. Diego was already grabbing an orange. Abuela said, "I am so sorry that I did not fix a snack for you *niños*, but I have been busy making flowers, a *piñata*, and some *luminarias*. I want this to be a beautiful party for our Paola!"

Diego asked, "Where is Paola?"

"Paola is at Amy's house. Remember?" Daisy answered. "She's spending the night with her best friend so we can get everything done for her birthday."

"Can she just move in over there?" Manuel asked. "I think one sister is enough! If we get rid of her and Daisy, then we will only have Carmen."

Daisy was making a bright yellow flower. She said, "If you get rid of us then every night will be the boys' night for dishes!"

Diego screamed, "Stop, Manuel! I hate doing the dishes!"

Abuela sighed, "Would you boys like to open the bags of candy, so we can fill the piñata?" They both shouted, "Yeah!"

Daisy knew her brothers would be eating some of the candy while they were dumping it into a giant metal bowl. She hoped they didn't eat it all.

Papi was bringing home some little toys to put in the piñata. Paola liked the little rings with big colorful glass in them. Daisy was too old now to get excited about the rings. Paola was just going to be eight years old, so she was still a little girl.

Abuela and Daisy put all of the flowers into three large plastic bags. Then Daisy set the table for dinner. Abuela had not had time to cook that day. So, Mami was bringing home pizza tonight. Ham with pineapple was Daisy's favorite kind. Her brothers liked pepperoni best.

When Mami and Papi got home, Mami would make a salad. Maybe her parents would let them sit on the floor and watch television while they ate. Usually they would say we eat our meal at the table, but with everyone so busy maybe they wouldn't care.

Daisy took her backpack to her room. She wanted to get all of her homework done that night so she would have the entire weekend to have fun. She opened her math book and began to solve the even problems on page 102.

She still had two problems to do when she heard the front door open. Papi loudly called for her brothers to help him get the bags of toys and birthday presents out of his truck. After a few minutes she heard Mami talking to Abuela. Soon it would be time to eat.

Daisy rushed to finish her math. Just as she was about to close her book, she heard Mami calling her. When she walked in the kitchen she noticed that her brothers were already begging.

"It's only pizza!" Manuel begged.

"We won't make a big mess. Promise!" Diego pleaded. "Please let us watch TV and eat!"

Papi put his arm around Mami and whispered in her ear. Mami looked unsure. She said, "Okay, but only tonight. Tomorrow we are all going to eat at the table. *Sí*?"

Daisy's brothers nodded in agreement. Then, they piled their plates with pizza and rushed to sit right in front of the TV.

Daisy took her time. Mami asked, "Daisy, how was your day?" Daisy told her mother all about the holiday reports they were doing in Ms. Lilly's class.

"Blanca and I got Halloween," Daisy said. "We think it's going to be fun. There is a whole section on trick-or-treating in the World Book."

"What are you going to be for Halloween, Daisy?" Papi asked.

Daisy described her idea for the Fall Festival. Then she said, "I might be a fortune-teller for Halloween."

25

"I have lots of shawls you can use," Abuela offered. "But you will need a pair of big gold earrings."

"Yeah, I know!" Daisy said. "I've been thinking of asking *Tia* Angie. She has lots of jewelry."

Abuela approved. She said, "That is a wonderful idea. We can call her right after we eat."

Daisy told her parents and her abuela that she hadn't even asked Ms. Lilly about it yet. All of the kids in room 210 would have to agree, and Madison wanted to have a bake sale.

Mami asked, "How are you going to get the food for the bake sale?"

Daisy replied, "It's not my problem! I don't want to have a boring bake sale. Blanca doesn't either. Besides, my idea is way better. It is perfect with Ms. Lilly being so mysterious."

Papi laughed and asked, "Are you going to use your Magic 8 Ball, mi ja?"

Daisy hadn't thought about it, but that was one way they could tell fortunes. A person could ask a question and the Magic 8 Ball would give the reply, but a real fortune-teller with a crystal ball would be much more exciting.

Daisy felt like the plan for the booth was crystallizing in her mind. She could hardly wait to call Blanca. As soon as she finished her pizza, she went to find the phone.

After a few rings, Blanca answered.

"Blanca, it's me," Daisy said. "I really think our idea for the fortune-telling booth could make room 210 famous!"

Blanca wanted Daisy to tell her the plan. Daisy explained, "We can make the entire room look like a fortune-telling tent. My tia Angie could loan us gold hoop earrings. Abuela said we can use some of her shawls. And Mami will loan us the gazing ball from her garden."

Blanca waited for Daisy to take a breath. She asked, "Are you sure this is our best idea?"

"Are you asking me if I have another idea?" Daisy asked. "I do, but I don't know if it's as good as the fortune-teller."

Blanca was wondering what the other idea could be. Daisy explained that Paola's piñata had given her an idea. It made her think about making calacas to put all around the room and skeleton skull piñatas. Kids could take a swing at the piñata for a ticket.

Blanca said, "Oooh! I love the calacas, but everyone has piñatas. We might not be the most popular booth at the festival if we do that."

Daisy wasn't so sure. She said, "Maybe we should tell our class both of the ideas we have."

Blanca agreed and then Daisy heard Blanca's mother telling her to hang up. She said, *"Buenas noches, amiga."*

It was time to get ready for bed, but Daisy didn't think she would sleep very much. She was too excited to sleep!

4
A Present Named Luna

Daisy woke up early the next morning. She rolled over and stretched. Then she saw her little black dog Noche sitting by the bed with a large pink tissue paper flower sticking out of her mouth.

"Noche, no!" Daisy yelled. She jumped out of bed and ran to the kitchen. The kitchen floor looked like a garden of beautiful pink, yellow, red, orange, purple, and green paper flowers. Noche still had the flower firmly clenched between her teeth.

"Oh no!" Daisy cried. "Noche, you are a bad little dog!" Pieces of the torn black garbage bags were scattered around, too. Then Manuel appeared in the door and began to laugh.

"It's not funny!" Daisy exclaimed. "Some of the flowers are ruined and we'll have to make more."

Before long Abuela, Diego, Mami, and Papi were all standing in the doorway. Papi said, "For being such a tiny dog, Noche sure knows how to make a big mess!"

Mami suggested Manuel and Diego help clean up. Daisy thought that was funny since Manuel was laughing at her earlier. Once all of the flowers were cleaned up, they all sat at the table and ate breakfast.

Mami began to give orders even before they finished eating. Papi would go get the balloons, Abuela would watch Carmen and help make the party bags, and Manuel and Diego would help Abuela. Daisy would make more flowers and a huge banner with *Happy Birthday, Paola* on it. Then, Mami would go to Tia Angie's house to make the food.

Tia Angie was making the *pastel*. It was going to have great big roses decorating it. The frosting would be very sweet, and the bright colors would make your mouth and teeth turn funny colors.

Everyone finished their jobs by lunchtime, but no one ate. They were busy loading everything up in Papi's truck to take to the park. When Daisy went to put some party bags on the front seat, she noticed a large box wrapped in pink paper with little holes in it.

Daisy leaned close and heard a tiny mewing sound. She spun around looking for Papi. He was coming out of the house.

"Papi, what is in the pink box?" Daisy yelled excitedly.

Papi said, "Sssh! It is a big surprise for your sister."

"Papi, if you have a kitten in the box it will be a big surprise for Paola, Mami, and Noche!" Daisy said. Papi grinned and put a finger over his lips.

As soon as they had everything loaded in the truck and Mami's car, they headed out to the park. At the park, they unloaded and put up decorations. Soon, a green van pulled in. It was Amy's mom bringing Paola and Amy to the party.

Paola jumped out to look at the paper streamers, flowers, balloons, banner, and piñata. She shouted, "It is so beautiful! I love my party. Thank you, Mami and Papi!"

Paola began hugging everyone. Then she saw the huge pile of wrapped presents. Mami said, "They are all for you, but you need to wait until later to open them. I see your friends are arriving so go and greet them."

Paola said, "Come on, Amy." The two girls went to stand by the first table. Before long, everyone had arrived. The party pavilion was crowded with kids from Ms. Wall's class, cousins, aunts, and uncles.

Daisy took Paola a plate. She said, "Hey, little sister, you better save room for cake. Tia Angie made it and it is chocolate."

"Yum!" Paola said. "I'll save room for two pieces."

Daisy was glad when Blanca finally arrived. "Hey, you're late!" she said. "This party has been a little boring. I'm glad you're here!"

The two girls headed for the food table, but Mami stopped them. She asked, "Daisy, can you please help with the piñata? I think we should do that now. Then we can have cake and Paola can open her presents."

Daisy replied, "Yes, Mami."

Blanca begged, "Can I please get some food first?"

Daisy laughed and said, "I guess. Meet me at the piñata, okay?"

Blanca agreed and ran off to get something to eat. Daisy went to put the blindfold on Paola. When she was ready, Daisy gave her the stick and spun her around. Paola swung and missed.

Everyone took a turn, and then another. Finally, Amy broke the piñata. Candy and little toys fell like rain onto the grass and all of the kids ran around picking them up.

"Blanca, did you see how much fun they had with the piñata?" Daisy asked. "Maybe we should change our mind about the fortune-telling."

"Yeah, they had fun," Blanca replied. "But both of our ideas are really good. Let's ask our class which is better. I'll be so bummed out if they choose Madison's bake sale."

Mami called Paola to blow out her candles. Then everyone at the party sang. Paola squeezed her eyes tight, took a huge breath, and blew out all of her candles.

"Mi ja, what did you wish for?" Abuela asked.

Paola shrugged and said, "I can tell you because I know it won't come true. I wished for a cat. Since Mami thinks one pet is enough, I can't have one. Still that's my wish."

Everyone had cake and ice cream. Finally it was time for presents. Paola tore into the packages. She opened more and more until only one gift was left on the table. It was the big pink box.

Mami looked suspiciously at Papi when he said, "This one is from me." He put the box in front of Paola.

Paola carefully opened the top. Then she screamed and jumped up and down. She shouted, "It's a kitten!" She lifted up a small, white ball of fluff so everyone could see.

"Is it a boy or a girl?" Paola asked.

Papi said, "It is a girl."

Abuela asked, "What will you name her?"

Paola thought for a minute. Then she kissed her new pet and announced, "This is Luna."

"That is a perfect name, Paola!" Daisy said. "When she is curled up she looks like a little moon."

Soon, parents began to arrive to pick up Paola's friends. Daisy and Blanca were busy cleaning up. The party was fun, and Paola seemed very happy.

On the way home Paola said, "Luna is my best present."

Daisy wondered if Noche and Luna would be friends. Then she thought, *Only one more day until Blanca and I can tell the class about our ideas for the Fall Festival.*

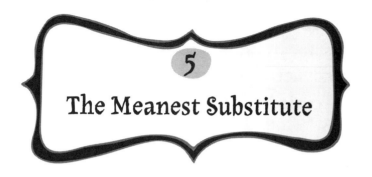

5
The Meanest Substitute

Monday morning, Mami called, "Daisy, Paola, Manuel, and Diego, wake up! Time to get ready for school."

Daisy didn't want to get up. It was hard to wake up Monday mornings, but today it was really hard. Daisy hadn't been able to fall asleep the night before because she was thinking about the Fall Festival. She couldn't wait to tell her class the best idea ever for their booth.

Daisy and Blanca had talked it over and they were going to tell their class two great ideas. But, she'd had another idea the night before. She'd decided they should make a calacas jack-o'-lantern, too.

Daisy could hear Paola getting dressed across the room. She opened her eyes and noticed her dog and her sister's new kitten, Luna, curled up on Paola's bed.

The night before, Papi had suggested that Noche sleep somewhere else. He was worried they wouldn't get along at first. But, Daisy decided that a cat and a dog could be friends, so she let her dog sleep in her bed.

During the night, Noche had jumped into Paola's bed with the little kitten. They seemed

to get used to each other right away. In fact, Noche was treating Luna just like a little sister.

Daisy dressed quickly. Today she added several wristbands to her outfit. She had a yellow one she bought at the mall to help find a cure for cancer. The rest were all for different charities. She had a red one, a pink one, and a red, white, and blue swirled one.

Downstairs at breakfast Mami asked if the family pets were getting along with each other. Paola nodded and said, "They are already best amigas. Last night they both slept on my bed."

As the kids grabbed their lunches off of the kitchen counter, Manuel told Daisy she had on too many wristbands.

"You look like an alien with a striped arm," he said. Daisy didn't bother to reply. She knew she looked amazing. Lots of girls had wristbands, but no one had been wearing them all at once. Daisy decided they looked neat.

The Martinez kids arrived at school just before the bell rang. By then, Daisy had been thinking about how she would tell her class the ideas she and Blanca had for the festival.

Finally, she knew that the best plan was to let Blanca tell about the calacas. She would explain about the fortune-teller. She was super excited as she turned the corner by room 210.

Something did not seem quite right. Kids were standing around in the hall. Daisy asked, "Why are we waiting out in the hall?"

Raymond explained that he had tried the door and it was locked. Suddenly the kids saw a tall, burly man with orange hair like carrots stomping toward them.

"I'm coming, I'm coming!" he shouted. "Move out of my way."

The kids parted and let him pass. He unlocked the door and motioned for them to go inside.

"Is that a substitute teacher?" Blanca asked.

Daisy replied, "I think so, but what's wrong with Ms. Lilly? Where is she?"

Raymond decided that she must be sick or she would be at school. He said, "She likes teaching us, so something is wrong with her or she would be here." Then he added, "Maybe a snake bit her."

Daisy was getting a sick feeling deep in her stomach. She liked Ms. Lilly. What if something bad happened and their teacher was not coming back?

The sub cleared his throat. He growled, "Your teacher is sick. I don't know if she will be back tomorrow, so don't ask me about it. Get out your notes for your holiday book project and get to work. If you need help, raise your hand."

Then he picked up his newspaper and began to read it. His name was on the board. It was Mr. Wright.

Some kids were talking quietly about their projects. Mr. Wright tossed his paper aside and yelled, "I told you to get to work. Be quiet!"

Daisy and Blanca began to work on their Halloween book. Blanca whispered, "Do you think he'll let us tell the class our plan?"

Daisy shook her head no. He seemed really mean. She whispered back, "We better talk about it in art class."

Everyone in room 210 worked quietly until Mr. Wright put down his paper and ordered the class to line up for art. Daisy decided she did not like substitute teachers—especially Mr. Wright, who seemed super mean.

In art, Daisy and Blanca talked while they worked on their projects. Using bright-colored paints, Daisy was working on a self-portrait.

To make her portrait, Daisy was using a picture her Papi had taken. Luckily her hair was in one long braid and she had tucked a large, red paper flower into it.

Daisy looked closely at the picture. She liked the soft curves of her cheeks and her glossy black hair. But it was still missing something.

Daisy decided to look at a painting of the artist Frida Kahlo with monkeys. It gave her an idea. She decided to put Noche in her painting, too.

After she'd made her decision, Daisy asked Blanca, "Do you think we should ask the sub about the plans for the festival? Or should we wait until Ms. Lilly comes back?"

"You ask," Blanca said. "He's scary."

Daisy shrugged. She said, "He creeps me out, too. But if we don't ask, Madison will get her way. We may end up with the boring bake sale."

Just then, Ms. Browner told the class to clean up. Daisy had to go rinse out her brushes.

Back in room 210, Daisy was trying to get over her nerves in order to ask Mr. Wright about the festival. Suddenly, Madison walked up to the teacher's desk and asked the substitute if they were still having the bake sale.

Mr. Wright said, "Sounds easy enough. Can you be in charge of it? I mean, getting the baked goods and making sure you have kids to sell them."

Madison smiled like she always did when she got her way. She said, "I sure can. I wouldn't want to let Ms. Lilly down, especially when she is feeling so sick."

The whole time Madison was talking at the teacher's desk, Daisy was feeling sick. Just what was Madison doing? Madison went back to her seat. Mr. Wright wrote Bake Sale for Fall Festival under his name.

Daisy gasped and Blanca moaned. No way! They didn't even get to tell any of the kids in their class about their fantastic idea.

A few minutes later, Madison passed around a sign-up sheet for her bake sale. It had a column for goodies and another for helpers. When she got it back there were only two names on the list—Lizzie and Amber.

Most of the class really didn't want to do a bake sale. Madison raised her hand, but Mr. Wright was reading his paper again and the class was supposed to be reading silently.

Finally, Madison called, "Mr. Wright, can I make an announcement about the bake sale?"

The teacher peered around his paper and nodded his approval.

"I have the sign-up sheet for the bake sale," Madison announced loudly. "I know you will all ask your parents tonight if you can bring a cake or some cookies or brownies. You can make your own or buy them from a bakery."

Right after that, Mr. Wright told them it was lunchtime.

6

Fish Sticks and Fortune-Telling

Daisy rushed to their table. She was frowning and looked really upset. Min said, "Daisy, what's wrong?"

Daisy grumbled, "Mr. Wright is wrong!"

Just then Blanca joined the table. She stared at the dry fish sticks on her tray. Then she commented, "This has to be the worst day ever! I hate fish!"

Raymond was at the other end of the table with a mountain of fish sticks on his tray. He was spraying them with ketchup.

He said, "I love fish sticks, I'll eat yours, too. I hope Ms. Lilly comes back tomorrow. That guy isn't even a real teacher. I don't think he likes kids."

Daisy pushed half of her lunch from home across the table for Blanca. She said, "Abuela to the rescue!" Blanca looked relieved. When she said she hated fish, she really meant it.

When the table filled up with kids Daisy asked, "Who wants the bake sale for our class booth?" No one said anything.

Finally Amber reminded them that they were already stuck with it, thanks to Madison.

Blanca suddenly smiled, "Maybe not. If no one signs up to bring baked goods, then we can't have a bake sale right?"

DeShaye said, "Oooh, girl, you've got an evil plan goin' on."

Daisy thought Blanca's idea was super smart. Raymond started to hiss like a snake *sssh, sssh*. All at once everyone stopped talking. They all looked up to see Madison walking over from across the cafeteria.

The room had large, rectangular tables arranged in rows down each side. Madison passed several tables. Then, she sat uninvited in the one empty chair at their table.

Madison said, "I just came over to see what you all are planning to bring for the bake sale."

DeShaye ignored Madison and said to Daisy, "Hey girl, where did you get all those wristbands? I like your style!"

Daisy held up her arm so everyone could see them. Madison looked at Daisy's wristbands.

Min said, "I love that idea. I'm going to wear all of mine tomorrow."

Blanca realized Madison was not leaving without an answer. Blanca muttered, "We'll let you know tomorrow." Madison seemed happy and stood up to go back to Lizzie and her friends.

Daisy told DeShaye her bracelet comment was a quick save. No one wanted Madison to know what they were really talking about. DeShaye thanked Daisy, but said she really did love her rainbow of bracelets.

Blanca looked around, her eyes following Madison across the cafeteria. She said, "It's okay to tell everyone about our plans."

Daisy leaned in to share their ideas about the piñatas or fortune-telling. All of the kids at the table got a little closer.

Just then, Principal Donaldson walked up. He said, "How's it going, kids?"

Min replied, "We are just great, Principal Donaldson." He gave them the thumbs-up and moved to another table.

Daisy asked Min for a pen. Then she drew a large skull on a napkin. She told the kids to imagine it as a piñata.

Blanca told them all about the calacas and said they could put them all around the room. Then they could hang the piñatas from the ceiling. The piñatas would be loaded with candy and treats.

Amber pointed out, "It sounds like fun, but wouldn't we need time to make the piñatas?

And who would pay for all of the stuff to go inside them?"

DeShaye agreed, "She's right, Daisy."

Blanca continued, "Okay, then tell them about our other idea."

Daisy told everyone about the fortune-telling idea she had. She told them that her abuela was going to help her with a costume. The best part of the fortune-telling plan was that it wouldn't cost anything. It also wouldn't take very long to decorate their room.

Min said, "I love your plan. Will you tell my fortune first?"

Several kids at the table wanted Daisy to read their fortunes, too! They thought her idea was totally cool. DeShaye told Daisy and Blanca they should go for it.

After lunch, Ms. Lilly's class went back to room 210 with Mr. Wright. When they walked into the room, the row of pumpkins along the wall made Daisy sadder than ever. They should be carving their pumpkins this afternoon, but Ms. Lilly was not there.

Instead, Mr. Wright asked Madison and Lizzie to pass out a worksheet. All afternoon they worked on their worksheets, but Daisy kept looking at the pumpkins.

Blanca kept looking at the clock. It seemed like the bell would never ring. Mr. Wright had finished reading the newspaper and was walking around the room. He had a stern look on his face.

Daisy was thinking if she had superpowers like Ms. Lilly then she would make the bell ring. Just then it did ring! Daisy started to load up her backpack. Blanca told her to hurry up. It seemed like all of the kids were ready to go home except Madison. She was talking to Mr. Wright again.

When Daisy got home, she told Abuela all about her terrible day. She really missed her teacher. She just wanted to forget all about school!

Abuela gave her a few dollars to go to the mini market and get a special snack. Manuel and Diego were mad.

"Oh man, no fair," Manuel complained. "Daisy always gets everything because she's the oldest."

Paola asked if she could go, too. Abuela told her no and passed out a snack.

Daisy was happy to have something to take her mind off of school. She quickly called

Blanca. Blanca rode her bike over so they could go to the store together.

The mini market was only a few blocks away. The girls talked as they walked. Daisy said, "Maybe we should think of some fortunes we could use."

Blanca liked the idea, but she thought they shouldn't tell anyone anything bad.

Daisy agreed, "Okay, only good stuff. Like I see an *A* in your future."

The mini market was busy that time of day, so the little store was crowded. People scooted past each other in the aisles.

Blanca wandered over to look at the candy. Daisy loved ice cream. She was by the frozen treats case when she noticed Raymond at the check-out counter.

Daisy pulled a cookies-and-cream ice cream sandwich out of the case. She thought Raymond might leave while she had her head in the case, but when she looked back up he was talking to Blanca.

Daisy walked over and Raymond said, "Hi, Daisy. That ice cream looks good. Maybe I'll get one, too."

"There's only one more left like this one," Daisy said. While Raymond was looking for the ice cream, Daisy and Blanca slipped out. They both needed to get home.

Before long it would be dinnertime, homework time, and then bed time. Daisy hoped Ms. Lilly would be back the next day!

7

Bake Sale Bomb

The kids from room 210 were disappointed when Ms. Lilly was sick again. Unfortunately, Mr. Wright was back! He barked out the assignments and then proceeded to read the newspaper.

Daisy whispered to Blanca, "When do you think Madison will ask about the bake sale?" She pointed at Madison, who was heading up to the teacher's desk at that very moment.

Blanca replied, "I think she is going to ask Mr. Wright right now!"

A few minutes later Madison announced, "Hey everyone, I'm passing around the sign-up sheet for the bake sale. I know it will be full when I get it back."

Daisy hoped it wouldn't be full. Blanca had been telling everyone that they should wait and help with the fortune-telling booth instead.

The sign-up sheet went up and down the rows until it had been all around the room. Daisy looked at Madison. She thought, *Any minute now she'll go* loco *when she finds out no one is bringing anything for the bake sale.*

When Madison looked at the almost empty sheet, her face turned red. She stood up and stomped her way to Ms. Lilly's desk.

Madison was pointing at the class, waving her hands around, and raising her voice. Mr. Wright didn't seem to care. Finally, he agreed to something.

Madison walked to the front of the room and announced, "I'm sure you didn't *all* forget to ask your parents about the bake sale!"

Raymond yelled, "You're right. We don't want to have a dumb bake sale. Face it, your bake sale bombed!"

This made Madison mad. She didn't like Raymond much anyway. Still, it seemed to be true since her sheet only had three names.

"Come on!" Madison begged. "This really is the best idea since Ms. Lilly is not here to help us."

Eric suggested that Ms. Lilly might be back tomorrow. That was when Mr. Wright finally decided to tell the class that Ms. Lilly would be back the next day!

Nearly all of the kids in room 210 had huge smiles on their faces. Well, not Madison. She was super angry now. Her plan was falling apart.

Mr. Wright stood up and said, "Since your teacher might be returning tomorrow, I'll let her deal with this mess. Now get back to work!"

Daisy felt sorry for Madison, who looked like she was about to cry. Madison seemed to calm down, but then a few minutes later asked for the bathroom pass.

Blanca said, "She's a crybaby just because she didn't get her way."

Daisy wasn't so sure that made Madison a crybaby. It was upsetting when no one wanted to go along with your idea. She and Blanca were lucky that most of the class wanted to go with the fortune-teller theme.

Just after Madison returned and hung the girls' bathroom pass, Mr. Wright told the class to line up for art. The kids in the line wanted to talk about Ms. Lilly coming back and the Fall Festival, but they were afraid of Mr. Wright. He was extra grouchy today.

Raymond was right. Mr. Wright didn't like kids much. When he dropped them off for art, he seemed happy for the first time that day.

Blanca asked, "What do you think he does while we are in art?"

"Probably drinks coffee and talks on his cell phone," Daisy replied.

Blanca was painting her clay pot. Daisy got her paints and made a palette. Then she painted some large green leaves around the edge of her self portrait. She added white to green and made light green leaves.

Soon, Raymond asked if he could have some of the paint she mixed for his frog carving.

Daisy said, "Sure, just take my palette and brush. I'm done for today."

Daisy looked at her painting. Ms. Browner asked, "Are you almost finished, Daisy? Don't forget, artists always sign their work."

Daisy had almost forgotten that part. She decided she would finish and sign her painting the next day. Art class was almost over and she still needed to get her palette and brushes back from Raymond to clean them up. She walked over to the table where he was working. His frog was really awesome.

"Raymond, maybe should add a little yellow and red on his back like a tree frog," Daisy suggested.

Raymond considered it. Finally, he approved. "I will, but my frog is a girl. I'm naming her Daisy."

Daisy realized that Raymond had already made up his mind. She took her supplies and went to clean them up.

Blanca was at the sink laughing. She said, "Wow, Daisy, you have a frog named in your honor."

Daisy warned, "Don't mention it!"

When they got back to class, Mr. Wright insisted, "Get out your books and read until lunchtime."

Everyone in the room sat quietly turning pages. Daisy was busy making lists in her head. She was not turning pages.

Soon, Mr. Wright came by her desk and jabbed his finger into her book. He hissed, "Are you reading?"

Daisy jumped and her eyes darted up in surprise. She said, "Uh-huh, I just got distracted."

Her book was good, but the festival plans kept creeping into her mind. She kept her eyes on her book to avoid another visit from the sub.

Finally it was time for lunch. Mr. Wright had them all line up to go to the cafeteria.

During lunch everyone talked about the fortune-telling booth and Madison got even madder. Amber was really excited because the school lunch today was her favorite, Frito Pie.

Raymond only ate one helping. He said, "I don't feel so good. My head is pounding and I am really warm. Is it hot in here?"

Blanca suggested, "Maybe you should go to the nurse."

Raymond looked at Daisy. She nodded in agreement. When Mr. Wright came to get them, Raymond asked to go to the nurse's office. He didn't come back to class.

After lunch, room 210 worked on their holiday books. The nurse came to get Raymond's backpack. She told Mr. Wright that Raymond had a fever and his mom was coming to get him.

Daisy wondered if he had the same thing Ms. Lilly did. Then she worried that she might get sick, too! Even Blanca looked concerned. Raymond was actually one of their friends now.

Daisy and Blanca were almost finished with their holiday book. They were glad when the bell rang and it was time to go home.

When Daisy got home, she called several kids in her class to see if they might want to help with the fortune-telling booth.

Finally, Abuela told Daisy it was time to get off the telephone and do her homework. Daisy went to her room to do her math homework. This time she had to do the odd problems.

Paola was doing her math, too. She was already at the desk they shared, so Daisy sat on the floor. Pretty soon Mami came home from working at the school. She peeked in the girls' room. Luna and Noche were on Paola's bed and both of the girls were busily working.

Mami said, "How was your day today?"

Paola replied, "Awesome! Everyone wants to know about Luna. Can I please take her picture to school?"

Mami agreed that Paola could take the photo to Ms. Wall's class.

Daisy said, "Not so good, Mami. Ms. Lilly was still sick and now Raymond is sick, too!"

Daisy was happy Ms. Lilly would be back the next day. Maybe she could think of a fun way to present her idea to Ms. Lilly and to the class.

8
Ms. Lilly Is Back!

Daisy didn't mind that lots of kids pointed at her as she zipped through the hall on her way to class. The night before, she had decided to wear a fortune-teller costume to present her idea to Ms. Lilly.

As she turned the corner, she ran into Blanca. Daisy squealed, "Hurry, Ms. Lilly is back today!"

Blanca didn't move. She looked at Daisy from top to bottom. Then she asked, "Aren't you wearing that costume too early? The festival isn't until Friday."

Daisy dashed around her friend. She wanted to get Ms. Lilly's approval for the booth. Blanca followed Daisy asking questions.

When they got to room 210, Ms. Lilly was sitting at her desk. Since she usually *never* sat down, they knew she was not feeling quite like herself yet.

Ms. Lilly smiled when she saw Daisy. Daisy had her long black hair loose with a scarf over it. She was wearing big gold hoop earrings, wrist bangles, a white top with a long purple skirt, and one of Abuela's colorful shawls.

"Oh my, Daisy!" Ms. Lilly said, "You look like a gypsy today. What is the special occasion?"

Daisy explained all about the fortune-telling booth. Kids kept coming up and interrupting Daisy to tell Ms. Lilly they missed her.

Their teacher listened and smiled. "I think we will have to discuss this with the class, Daisy," Ms. Lilly said.

After the bell rang, Ms. Lilly presented Daisy's fortune-telling idea. Madison was mad. Her face looked like a thunder cloud. Her hand shot straight up.

"Madison, do you have something to add?" Ms. Lilly asked.

Madison responded, "I thought we were using my idea to have a bake sale."

Ms. Lilly decided the only fair thing to do was to let the class vote. She wrote in big curly black letters *Fortune-telling* on one side of the board and *Bake Sale* on the other side.

Finally she asked, "All those in favor of the fortune-telling booth please raise your hand?"

Ms. Lilly began to count then stopped suddenly. She seemed surprised, "Where is Raymond? He is always here."

Blanca offered, "He got sick yesterday and had to go home."

Ms. Lilly kept counting. Then she told the students who wanted the bake sale to raise their hands. There were only five, including Madison.

Ms. Lilly sat back down. She said, "Fortune-telling it is then!"

Daisy was glad she had worn the costume and called kids the night before, too. The class began to plan their booth.

Ms. Lilly divided them up into groups. She had one group for setting up. There was another group for writing fortunes. A third group would be in charge of taking tickets. A fourth group would do the actual fortune-telling. And a final group would clean up.

When everything was settled, Ms. Lilly asked them to put the finishing touches on their holiday books.

Daisy went to Ms. Lilly's desk and asked, "If Raymond is back to school tomorrow, can he be in my group? I'm sorry he is so sick. He was really excited about this idea."

Ms. Lilly agreed. Then Madison raised her hand again. "I think I should be in the fortune-telling group," she suggested.

Ms. Lilly was not convinced. She said since it was Daisy and Blanca's idea, they would be the fortune-tellers. Then she told Madison that she really needed her to be in charge of writing fortunes because she was such a terrific writer. This satisfied Madison.

Room 210 zoomed into high gear to get everything ready in record time. It was great having Ms. Lilly back! She even let them carve their jack-o'-lanterns.

On Thursday, the class put the covers on their holiday books. Daisy and Blanca's looked like a brown paper sack. The title was Trick-or-Treat: A Book about Halloween.

Ms. Lilly loved it. She said, "I have super creative students. I can't wait to get them into our library."

Then she told them to work in their groups for the fortune-telling booth. Daisy and Blanca talked about their costumes and made a list of things they would need.

Madison and her group were busy reading the fortunes they were writing. Madison handed one to Daisy that said, "You will get sick and miss the festival." Then she laughed.

"I hope not!" Daisy said. Then she thought about Raymond. Daisy hoped he wouldn't miss all the fun!

9

Festival Fortune-Tellers

When Daisy woke up on Friday, Abuela was making churros for Paola's class to sell at the festival. The whole house smelled like cinnamon.

Daisy jumped out of bed, calling to Paola to get up. Noche chased after her. Luna followed Noche. Paola followed Luna. They looked like a little parade on the way to the bathroom.

After they were all dressed, they went to eat breakfast.

Paola bragged, "Everyone will smell Abuela's tasty churros and come to Ms. Wall's class to spend their tickets."

Diego said, "I like the dunking booth the best. Principal Donaldson is taking a turn."

Manuel added, "I like the jail. All I have to do is give the sheriff a ticket and he will put you in jail, Diego. You better save some tickets so you can get out!" The kids grabbed their lunches and headed to school.

Room 210 was almost ready. The group setting up had covered the walls with black paper and draped shawls around one side of the room. They had two big, round tables with black cloths and large, clear globes on them.

Raymond was back at school, but he seemed a little tired. Daisy told him that he was a part of the fortune-telling group. His job would be to sit inside the door and tell people to go to Lady Blanca or Madame Daisy for their fortune.

The class soon finished all of its preparations. After lunch, Ms. Lilly's students presented their holiday books to the class. Then it was time to go home. They would be coming back in a few short hours for the festival!

At the Martinez house, everyone was excited about the festival. Abuela was packing up the churros. Mami and Papi were going to help with the ticket sales. Tia Angie was going to babysit Carmen.

The boys were running around the house in their monster costumes. Paola was helping Daisy get ready. Daisy was already wearing her costume, but she had painted her fingernails red and the polish was still wet. Paola took the long braid out of Daisy's hair.

Pretty soon, Mami and Papi loaded the churros, the children, and Abuela into the van. At the school, the Martinez family was greeted by chaos. People were running in every direction. Someone shouted, "We need a table for ticket sales!" Papi went to help.

The boys asked, "Can we have our ticket money now, Mami?" Soon they would be trying to get someone wet in the dunking booth or put each other in jail. Mami handed them some dollar bills. They counted them, smiled, and took off for the gym.

Abuela and Paola were taking the churros to Ms. Wall's room. Daisy headed for room 210.

Blanca was waiting at one of the fortune-telling tables. She said, "Daisy, your eyes look like black pools! You should wear makeup all the time. You look beautiful and mysterious!"

Daisy explained to Blanca that she didn't need it. She thought she usually looked fabulous anyway. Daisy knew her caramel-colored skin was smooth, clear, and lovely.

Raymond arrived to stand at the door. He was wearing all black clothes with a long black cape. In his hand he held a black top hat.

The second Raymond saw Daisy he was speechless! A minute later he announced, "You look amazing, Daisy!" He couldn't take his eyes off of her.

Blanca warned him, "Raymond, you're staring!"

Daisy laughed and said, "You look mysterious in your black cape too, Raymond." Just then people began to line up. It was five o'clock and time for the Fall Festival to begin.

Raymond shouted, "Step right up! Get your fortune told by the mysterious Madame Daisy or the all-knowing Lady Blanca!"

Madison's team had written lots of fortunes on small cards that Daisy and Blanca kept in their laps. They sat down at their tables.

Daisy looked around. She saw the dark walls covered with the colorful shawls. Their long fringe made a curtain in the eerie glow of the candlelight from the jack-o'-lanterns. They were ready!

Daisy's first customer was Amber. She said, "Welcome. Do you wish to know what lies in your future?"

Amber giggled, "Yes, Madame Daisy, I do!"

Daisy waved her hands over the crystal ball. She said, "I see something." Then she looked at the card she pulled from her lap. She continued, "You will have an exciting adventure very soon."

Amber giggled again, "Madame Daisy, how did you know? You're right. I am going to the dunking booth next!"

Daisy tried to look more mysterious. She said, "I have a gift, a special power to see things." She was trying not to laugh. She could not hear Blanca. They agreed earlier to whisper. That way they would not be talking over each other.

After Amber, Daisy read fortunes for Eric, Ms. Lilly, and Min. Blanca got DeShaye, Coach Cervantes, and Ms. Browner. People kept coming all evening. It was so busy that Daisy and Blanca could not even take a break.

Pretty soon Madison and Lizzie came in.
Daisy got Madison. It was a good thing. Blanca
was a little mean to her sometimes, but she said
she deserved it. Daisy waved her hands over
the crystal ball.

Madison demanded, "Come on already, just
tell me what the card says."

Daisy replied, "Okay, I thought you wanted
the whole fortune-telling experience. She

pulled a card out. The she read, "You will be a star student."

Madison snorted, "Tell me something I don't know, Daisy!" She pushed back her chair and minutes later someone else sat down.

Finally, Principal Donaldson said over the loud speaker, "Thank you everyone for coming and making the Fall Festival a huge success. It is nine o'clock. The festival is over. See you next year!"

Ms. Lilly was counting the tickets in the hall. Daisy heard her talking to her Mami. She said, "Mrs. Martinez, your Daisy is such a creative girl. Our booth has been the most popular one at the festival. Daisy is a superstar!"

Papi told Mami he had a candy apple for Daisy. Mami said, "Oh Jorge, she will be so happy. Candy apples are her favorite!"

Before they started to clean up the classroom Blanca called, "Daisy, come and let me read your fortune!"

It was still dark in room 210. Raymond came to the table, too. Blanca leaned over as if in a trance. She waved her hands over the clear glowing ball. She said, "I see something . . . something a little dark and mysterious. Do you want to see into your future?"

Daisy laughed, "Yes, I do."

Blanca looked at the card and then at Daisy and Raymond. She seemed puzzled. She said, "I was only joking around."

Raymond begged, "Read the card, Lady Blanca!"

Blanca looked at her best friend. She asked, "Daisy, are you sure?" Daisy nodded. Blanca read, "Be prepared. Sadness and trouble will soon visit you."

Spanish Glossary

abuela – grandmother

amiga – friend

buenas noches – good night

churros – crispy cinnamon treat

el dia de la muerta – the day of the dead

fiesta – party

loco – crazy

luminarias – lights

mi ja – my dear

niños – children

pastel – a type of cake

piñata – a decorated container filled
with candy and gifts and hung
up to be broken
with sticks

sí – yes

tia – aunt

tonta – silly